I Can Make A Difference

A TREASURY TO INSPIRE OUR CHILDREN

SELECTED BY

 MARIAN WRIGHT EDELMAN

ILLUSTRATIONS BY BARRY MOSER

 HarperCollins*Publishers*

Amistad

To all my grandchildren and their children through all the generations with enduring love. It is also dedicated to all those who work tirelessly to raise, empower, and build nations and a world where no child is left behind and everyone belongs.
—M.W.E.

And for my newest grandson, Jackson Chase Harper
—B.M.

ACKNOWLEDGMENTS
Deep thanks to Lisa Clayton Robinson, Kathy Tindell,
Martha Espinosa, and Kara Vicinelli for their help in putting this book together.
I am always grateful for the gracious silent spaces provided
by my friends Deborah Szekely and Carol Biondi. —M.W.E.

Amistad is an imprint of HarperCollins Publishers Inc.
I Can Make a Difference
Compilation copyright © 2005 by Marian Wright Edelman
Illustrations copyright © 2005 by Barry Moser
Acknowledgments of permission to reprint previously published material
appear on pages 110–112.

Manufactured in China.
Library of Congress Cataloging-in-Publication Data is available.
ISBN 0-06-028051-4 — ISBN 0-06-028052-2 (lib. bdg.)

Typography by Stephanie Bart-Horvath
1 2 3 4 5 6 7 8 9 10
❖
First Edition

CONTENTS

Introduction 5

1. I can make a difference by loving myself and others as God loves us and treating others respectfully and fairly. 9

2. I can make a difference by being courageous. 15

3. I can make a difference by aiming high and holding on to my ideals. 21

4. I can make a difference by caring and serving. 25

5. I can make a difference by being honest and telling the truth. 35

6. I can make a difference by persevering and not giving up. 43

7. I can make a difference by being determined and resourceful. 51

8. I can make a difference by being grateful for the gift and wonders of life. 59

9. I can make a difference by working together with others. 67

10. I can make a difference by being compassionate and kind. 75

11. I can make a difference by being nonviolent and working for peace. 85

12. I can make a difference by being faithful and struggling for what I believe. 97

Introduction

WHAT KIND of people do we want to be? What kind of people do we want our children to be? What kind of moral examples, teachings, choices—personal, community, and political—are we parents, grandparents, and community adults prepared to make at this turn of the century and millennium to make our children strong inside and empowered to seek and help build a more just, compassionate, and less violent society and world?

Over two thousand years ago, a Palestinian Jew named Jesus taught that "Man shall not live by bread alone." His message is in danger of being lost as so many of our children of privilege and poverty chase material idols that fade, and stuff themselves with the cultural junk foods of violence, drugs, and material things that fail to fill the deeper hunger for community and purpose all humans share.

The twentieth century was characterized by stunning scientific and technological progress. We split the atom, pierced space, walked on the moon, landed on Mars, and broke the genetic code. Instant communication led to an information explosion and daily money trading in the trillions. We witnessed astonishing increases in wealth resulting from a tiny microchip. We can fly through the air faster than the speed of sound and cruise the seas quicker than the creatures inhabiting them. We created the capacity to feed the world's population and to prevent the poverty that afflicts the majority of humankind. But something is missing. Our scientific and military progress have not been accompanied by comparable moral progress.

Every child today is infected by our violence-saturated culture and excessive consumerism. Buying is equated with happiness. Possessing things is equated with success. Children are marketed sex, alcohol, tobacco, and violence as the way to be accepted.

I believe the prophets, the Gospels, the Koran, other great faiths, history, moral decency, and common sense beckon us to examine anew as individuals and as a people what we are to live by and teach our children. Parents, grandparents, teachers, preachers, neighbors, people of conscience, and people of faith must lift a strong counter voice to the corrupting messages of our culture and teach our children that they can make a difference.

Making a difference is the organizing framework for this book. I believe each of us is put on this earth for a purpose and with the duty to make this world a better place. My parents and Black community elders taught, by word and deed, that service is the rent each of us pays for living and that the only thing that lasts is what is shared with others. They passed down the habit of service and created opportunities for children to serve at very young ages. They also taught that service and charity are not enough—that we have to raise our voices for justice and freedom also. If we don't like the way the world is, we can do our part to change it. Success is never guaranteed, but contributing to the struggle is a responsibility and a privilege.

How can we make a difference? In this book, I have selected twelve essential ways in which children can make a difference in their lives and in the lives of those around them. I have chosen quotes, stories, and poems from cultures around the world to illustrate these twelve values and to inspire the children and parents who read them together.

The principles outlined in this book are:

1. I can make a difference by loving myself and others as God loves us and treating others respectfully and fairly.
2. I can make a difference by being courageous.
3. I can make a difference by aiming high and holding on to my ideals.
4. I can make a difference by caring and serving.
5. I can make a difference by being honest and telling the truth.

6. I can make a difference by persevering and not giving up.

7. I can make a difference by being determined and resourceful.

8. I can make a difference by being grateful for the gift and wonders of life.

9. I can make a difference by working together with others.

10. I can make a difference by being compassionate and kind.

11. I can make a difference by being nonviolent and working for peace.

12. I can make a difference by being faithful and struggling for what I believe.

I hope this book will inspire and empower children through the stories and wisdom of the many cultures and peoples with whom our children must share a world. All our children need to know that goodness and wisdom come in all colors and countries and genders and sizes and do not belong to any single person or group or nation. I also hope this book will help build children strong on the inside, with spiritual anchors to meet challenges with resiliency, knowing always what Ralph Waldo Emerson said: "What lies behind us and what lies before us are tiny matters compared to what lies within us."

We can all make a difference.

1.

I can make a difference

by loving myself and others as

God loves us and treating

others respectfully and fairly.

PEOPLE OF different religions and beliefs disagree on many things. But all major religions agree on treating your neighbor—who is all other human beings—as you would like to be treated.

Every major religion teaches us to love each other as ourselves.

Christianity—All things whatsoever you would that others should do to you, do you even so to them.

Judaism—Thou shalt love thy neighbor as thyself.

Islam—No one of you is a believer until he loves for his brother what he loves for himself.

Hinduism—Good people proceed while considering what is best for others is best for themselves.

Zoroastrianism—Whatever is disagreeable to yourself do not do to others.

Buddhism—Hurt not others with that which pains yourself.

Confucianism—What you do not want done to yourself do not do unto others.

Taoism—Regard your neighbor's gain as your own gain, and regard your neighbor's loss as your own loss.

I have a dream that my four little children will one day live in a nation where they will not be judged by the color of their skin but by the content of their character.

—The Rev. Dr. Martin Luther King, Jr.

Dear Dr. King,

We could sure use your help nowadays. Not only has segregation between Blacks and Whites started again, but now some people are rude in helping people of their own color. . . . Many of the handicapped and disabled children only have each other, because people think they have something that others can catch and it caused them to become that way. Children in schools pick their friends, and many of the "strange ones," as they would put it, don't get picked.

—Kimberly, age 11

Each second we live in a new and unique moment of the universe, a moment that never was before and will never be again. And what do we teach our children in school? We teach them that two and two make four, and that Paris is the capital of France. When will we also teach them what they are? We should say to each of them: Do you know what you are? You are a marvel. You are unique. In all of the world there is no other child exactly like you. In the millions of years that have passed there has never been another child like you. And look at your body—what a wonder it is! your legs, your arms, your cunning fingers, the way you move! You may become a Shakespeare, a Michelangelo, a Beethoven. You have the capacity for anything. Yes, you are a marvel. And when you grow up, can you then harm another who is, like you, a marvel? You must cherish one another. You must work—we all must work—to make this world worthy of its children.

—*Pablo Casals*

A Love Poem to Every Special Child

Black and Brown girl dark of hue with kinky or curly hair

White child with straight hair and freckles too

God painted your skin and curled and straightened your hair just for you.

God is love and you are God's beloved.

Black, Brown, Yellow, Red, and White child created to look just like you,
      God rejoices and is glad in you.

God is love and you are God's beloved.

Special child who sees and discerns without the eyes and ears and speech the rest
      of us need

who navigates without the legs ordinary people require and manages without
      the hands on which other mortals depend.

God is love and you are God's beloved.

Weary child of the night and castaway of the streets afraid and abused

in need of safe haven and home to rest and to nest.

God is love and you are God's beloved.

Child of slow mind, innocent of worldly wiles and the will to harm others, freed
      of devious thoughts.

God is love and you are God's beloved.

Child of poverty unburdened by the chains of things and greed which imprison
      the haves too muches.

God came in your disguise to save us all.

God is love and you are God's beloved.

—Marian Wright Edelman

Just Me

Nobody sees what I can see,
For back of my eyes there is only me.
And nobody knows how my thoughts begin,
For there's only myself inside my skin.
Isn't it strange how everyone owns
Just enough skin to cover his bones?
My father's would be too big to fit—
I'd be all wrinkled inside of it.
And my baby brother's is much too small—
It just wouldn't cover me up at all.
But I feel just right in the skin I wear,
And there's nobody like me anywhere.

—*Margaret Hillert*

2.

I can make a difference

by being courageous.

You gain strength, courage, and confidence by every
experience in which you really stop to look fear in the face. . . .
You must do the thing you think you cannot do.

—*Eleanor Roosevelt*

Life Doesn't Frighten Me

SHADOWS ON the wall
Noises down the hall
Life doesn't frighten me at all
Bad dogs barking loud
Big ghosts in a cloud
Life doesn't frighten me at all.

Mean old Mother Goose
Lions on the loose
They don't frighten me at all
Dragons breathing flame
On my counterpane
That doesn't frighten me at all.

I go boo
Make them shoo
I make fun
Why they run
I won't cry
So they fly
I just smile
They go wild
Life doesn't frighten me at all.

Tough guys in a fight
All alone at night
Life doesn't frighten me at all.

Panthers in the park
Strangers in the dark
No, they don't frighten me at all.

That new classroom where
Boys all pull my hair
(Kissy little girls
With their hair in curls)
They don't frighten me at all.

Don't show me frogs and snakes
And listen for my scream,
If I'm afraid at all
It's only in my dreams.

I've got a magic charm
That I keep up my sleeve,
I can walk the ocean floor
And never have to breathe.

Life doesn't frighten me at all
Not at all
Not at all.
Life doesn't frighten me at all.

—Maya Angelou

Li Chi and the Serpent

ONCE, IN ANCIENT days, in the Kingdom of Yueh, a terrible serpent came to live in the Yung Mountains. There it coiled around the rocks and sent dreadful dream messages to everyone—*I will destroy the land and all the people if I am not given maidens to eat.*

Oh, the wailing and moaning that followed the hearing of this threat. What could the people possibly do?

"We can't let our maidens be eaten!" they cried.

So the people sent for brave heroes to kill the serpent for them. The heroes swaggered boldly up to the mountain peak. But when they saw the serpent, with its terrible fangs and claws, every one of those heroes ran away.

"Enough delay!" the serpent roared at the people. "I will destroy you all if I am not given maidens to eat, and quickly!"

"What can we do now?" the people wailed. "We have no heroes left! We will surely have to give the serpent the maidens it wishes."

And so, a hunt for maidens began. Word of this dreadful search reached the family of a poor farmer, Li Tan. Li Tan had once been a soldier, but that had been long ago. Now he was a father with six daughters, and his old sword hung on the wall, slowly rusting.

When Li Tan and his daughters heard about the serpent, they began to weep at the thought that one of them might well be chosen to be eaten.

Only the youngest of the six daughters, Li Chi, did not waste time weeping. "Why should I cry about something that might never happen?" she told her father. "And I refuse to let myself be frightened of a creature that I have never seen!"

Instead, Li Chi began to wonder just how such a monster might be stopped. And an idea came to her.

"Let me be chosen," she told her father.

"No!" he cried in horror.

"Yes," she insisted. "Only be sure the officials who come for me give you a nice ransom in exchange for me. That way, no matter what happens, my sisters will have some money on which to live. Oh, Father, don't worry. I have no intention of letting myself be eaten. And I have no intention of letting any other girls be eaten either!"

The officials came for her very soon. "I will come with you," Li Chi said humbly. "But first, let me take a memory of home with me."

So she took her father's rusty sword, the farm's snake-hunting dog, and a sack of sweet rice with her. She let the officials lead her up to the mountain peak. There, Li Chi seated herself comfortably and began rolling the sweet rice into tasty treats. These she placed at the entrance of the serpent's cave. Then she hid in the shadows to wait, holding the snake-hunting dog so that he would not whine or bark.

The serpent smelled the sweet rice and came out of the cave. Oh, but he was terrible to see with teeth sharp as spears and eyes bright and fierce as flames. Hiding in the shadows, Li Chi bit her lip to keep from crying out in fear.

The serpent paused, looking down at the sweet rice. *What is this? These strange objects smell interesting, indeed!* After a wary look around, he lowered his head and began to eat.

"Now!" Li Chi whispered to the dog, and let him loose. The serpent smelled just like a snake to the dog, and he bit the monster with all his might. The serpent roared in surprise and whirled toward the dog—and as he did, he left his long neck exposed. Li Chi raised her father's sword and struck down with all her strength, cutting that serpent's head right off.

"You will never eat another maiden," Li Chi said, and went home.

Word of Li Chi's feat reached the King of Yueh. He went to visit her father's farm. He liked what he saw of Li Chi so much—and she liked what she saw of him, too—that he made her his queen. She and all her family lived happily at court from then on.

And no other monsters ever troubled the Kingdom of Yueh again.

—A tale from China

3.

I can make a difference

by aiming high and

holding on to my ideals.

No pessimist ever discovered the secret of the stars, or sailed to an uncharted land, or opened a new doorway for the human spirit.

—*Helen Keller*

If you have built castles in the air, your work need not be lost; that is where they should be. Now put the foundations under them.

—*Henry David Thoreau*

It must be borne in mind that the tragedy of life doesn't lie in not reaching your goal. The tragedy lies in having no goal to reach. It isn't a calamity to die with dreams unfulfilled, but it is a calamity not to dream.
It is not a disaster to be unable to capture your ideal, but it is a disaster to have no ideal to capture. It is not a disgrace not to reach the stars, but it is a disgrace to have no stars to reach for. Not failure, but low aim is sin.

—*Dr. Benjamin E. Mays*

If You Think You Are Beaten

IF YOU THINK you are beaten, you are;
If you think that you dare not, you don't;
If you'd like to win, but you think you can't,
It's almost a cinch that you won't.

If you think you'll lose, you've lost;
For out in the world you'll find
Success begins with a person's will,
It's all in the state of mind.

Full many a race is lost
Ere even a step is run,
And many a coward falls
Ere even his work's begun.

—*Anonymous*

Listen to the Mustn'ts

Listen to the MUSTN'TS, child,
Listen to the DON'TS
Listen to the SHOULDN'TS
The IMPOSSIBLES, the WON'TS
Listen to the NEVER HAVES
Then listen close to me—
Anything can happen, child,
ANYTHING can be.

—*Shel Silverstein*

Speech to the Young
Speech to the Progress-Toward

For Nora Brooks Blakely
For Henry Blakely III

Say to them,
say to the down-keepers,
the sun-slappers,
the self-foilers,
The harmony-hushers,
"Even if you are not ready for day
it cannot always be night."
You will be right.
For that is the hard home-run.

And remember:
live not for Battles Won.
Live not for The-End-of-the-Song.
Live for the along.

—*Gwendolyn Brooks*

Sojourner Truth

4.

I can make a difference

by caring and serving.

How lovely to think that no one need wait a moment,
we can start now, start slowly changing the world!

—*Anne Frank*

Facing a heckler once who told her he did not care for her antislavery talk
any more than he would for the bite of a flea, Sojourner Truth retorted,
"Perhaps not, but Lord willing, I'll keep you scratching."

A Prayer for Each of Us to Serve

LORD, I cannot preach like Martin Luther King, Jr.
or turn a poetic phrase like Maya Angelou
but I care and am willing to serve.

I do not have Fred Shuttlesworth's and
Harriet Tubman's courage
or Eleanor and Franklin Roosevelt's political skills
but I care and am willing to serve.

I cannot sing like Fannie Lou Hamer
or organize like Ella Baker and Bayard Rustin
but I care and am willing to serve.

I am not holy like Archbishop Tutu,
forgiving like Mandela, or disciplined like Gandhi
but I care and am willing to serve.

I am not brilliant like Dr. Du Bois or
Elizabeth Cady Stanton,
or as eloquent as Sojourner Truth and
Booker T. Washington
but I care and am willing to serve.

I have not Mother Teresa's saintliness,
Dorothy Day's love or
Cesar Chavez's gentle tough spirit
but I care and am willing to serve.

God, it is not as easy as the 60s
to frame an issue and forge a solution
but I care and am willing to serve.

My mind and body are not so swift as in youth
and my energy comes in spurts
but I care and am willing to serve.

I'm so young
nobody will listen
I'm not sure what to say or do
but I care and am willing to serve.

I can't see or hear well
speak good English, stutter sometimes
and get real scared standing up before others
but I care and am willing to serve.

Use me as Thou will to save Thy children today and tomorrow
and to build a nation and world where no
child is left behind and everyone feels welcome.

—Marian Wright Edelman

Holding Up the Sky

ONE DAY an elephant saw a hummingbird lying
on its back with its tiny feet up in the air. "What
are you doing?" asked the elephant.

The hummingbird replied,
"I heard that the sky might fall today,
and so I am ready to help hold it up,
should it fall."

The elephant laughed cruelly.
"Do you really think," he said,
"that those tiny feet could help hold up the sky?"

The hummingbird kept his feet up in the air,
intent on his purpose, as he replied,
"Not alone. But each must do what he can.
And this is what I can do."

— *A tale from China*

WHAT ACTIONS are
most excellent?

To gladden the heart
of a human being.
To feed the hungry.
To help the afflicted.
To lighten the sorrow
of the sorrowful.
To remove the wrongs
of the injured.
That person is the
most beloved of God
who does most good
to God's creatures.

—*The Prophet Muhammed*

The Generous Physician

GENEROUS EVEN IN THOUGHT WAS ABBA UMANA,
WHO DISARMED CRITICISM BY NOT MAKING USE OF IT.

ABBA UMANA was a physician who had attained great celebrity, so that he was known as Father, or Chief, of the Skillful. His fame was further amplified by tales of his generosity.

For instance, he was most considerate of a patient's pride. He would not name a fee, lest it be more than the sick person could afford. He had a box set up in a private corner of his house, where those who came to him for advice and treatment would deposit whatever they could pay. If without means, they need not be put to shame, while the rich could give genuine proof of their gratitude.

It worked out very well for Abba Umana. He was able to live comfortably; and the report of his magnanimity spread beyond his own land.

It spread to faraway Babylonia, where Abbayé was head of the Talmudic academy. Two of his pupils were sick and seemed to make no progress under the treatment of neighboring physicians. Abbayé sent for them. "You shall go, my sons," he said, "to Abba Umana. Money for the journey will be provided, and for your lodging in the town until, God willing, you be cured. In the meantime, satisfy my curiosity about that saintly man. See if he is really as generous and good as they say."

The students set out. When they came to Abba Umana, he diagnosed their ailment and said: "You must come to me every day for treatment. Meanwhile, as students journeying from so far away, you shouldn't be allowed to waste your money paying for lodgings. Stay in my house and be my guests until you recover. You will be welcome. There's nothing I like better than hearing about travel and foreign lands and different customs."

As for putting money in the box, Abba Umana would not hear of it. "I should pay *you*," he said, "for the pleasure of your company!"

The students spent several days in great comfort at Abba Umana's house. They joined him at meals, while he listened delightedly to their college gossip and drew them out about their teachers and the government of the community. They shared an excellent room and enjoyed the sights of the city.

In short they felt an increasing unwillingness to make trial of their kind host's generosity. They already knew him as the finest person they had ever met. Still, to obey the request of the fatherly Abbayé, they planned to put their doctor to a test.

When he told them they were cured but asked them to remain with him a day or two longer, they thanked him and assented.

Before dawn on the following morning, without a word or message of farewell, they stole out of the house, taking with them the rich silken tapestry that had covered their bed. They took their stand in the marketplace at a spot where they knew Abba Umana must pass in his daily routine, and offered the coverlet for sale.

As the physician came up to them, they shamelessly displayed it and asked him what he would pay for it. "Seven gold pieces," said

Abba Umana amiably. "At least, that is what I paid for a coverlet very much like it." And to their amazement, he took that sum from his purse and gave it to them.

"But do you not see," exclaimed one of the students, not closing his hand on the gold, "that this is your own property?"

"We stole it from your house," cried the other youth. "Aren't you going to call us thieves—and—and ingrates?"

Abba Umana laughed indulgently. "You must have a good reason for what you are doing. From what I have seen of you, you cannot be thieves. It may be you have a righteous purpose in mind. Perhaps you want to raise money for a special good deed, such, for instance, as buying a Jewish slave or captive in order to release him, and are merely ashamed to say so."

"Our only purpose," they told him, "was to put your generosity and faith in humankind to the test. And we're content. All the praise that has been given you is well deserved!"

"What flattery is this that you pour into an old man's ears!" the physician rejoined. He would not accept the coverlet. "I have enough of such things," he said. "Besides, in my mind I knew you had good intentions and I already devoted it to a charitable purpose. Consequently, it is no longer mine."

"But we have no place for it," the students insisted. "It is far too handsome for our use."

"Sell it, then, and divide the money among the poor." Abba Umana sighed. "Look about you! There are far too many who need it!"

That was the satisfying story they brought back to Abbayé.

—A traditional Jewish tale

IF I CAN stop one Heart from breaking
I shall not live in vain
If I can ease one Life the Aching
Or cool one Pain

Or help one fainting Robin
Unto his Nest again
I shall not live in Vain.

—*Emily Dickinson*

5.

I can make a difference

by being honest

and telling the truth.

Once to every man and nation comes the moment to decide,
In the strife of Truth with Falsehood, for the good or evil side.

—James Russell Lowell

Fire, Water, Truth, and Falsehood

Long ago, Fire, Water, Truth, and Falsehood lived together in one large house. They were considerate of one another, but tried to stay out of one another's way. Truth and Falsehood sat as far apart as they could, and Fire stayed out of Water's way.

One day the four housemates went hunting together. They found a herd of cattle and began driving them home. Truth spoke up and said, "Let us divide the cattle equally among us, for that is the only fair way." No one disagreed.

But as they walked, Falsehood decided that it would be better to have more than an even share of the cattle, and so Falsehood went over to Water and said, "You are more powerful than Fire. Destroy Fire, and there will be more cattle for all of us."

Water flowed over to Fire, who soon went out in a steaming burst of smoke. Now there were only three.

Falsehood whispered to Truth, "Look how Water has destroyed Fire. Let's leave Water and go high into the mountains so our cattle can graze."

Higher and higher they climbed, and since water cannot flow upward, it could not follow. Water washed down the slope, as it does to this day.

When Truth and Falsehood reached the mountaintop, Falsehood turned on Truth and said, "I am more powerful than you! You are now my servant. I am your master. All the cattle belong to me!"

But Truth would not agree. "I will never be your servant!" he cried.

They fought bitterly until finally they decided to bring their argument to Wind. Wind would decide who the master was. But Wind didn't know. Wind blew all over the world, asking people whether Truth or Falsehood was more powerful. Some people said, "A single word of Falsehood can destroy Truth." Others said, "Like a small candle in the dark, one word of Truth can change everything."

Wind listened carefully to what everyone had to say and returned with an answer. Wind said, "I see now that Falsehood is very powerful. But it can only rule where Truth has stopped struggling to be heard."

—An Ethiopian tale from northeast Africa

Feathers

A sharp-tongued woman was accused
of starting a rumor. When she
was brought before the village
rabbi, she said, "I was only
joking. My words were spread by
others, and so I am not to blame."
But the victim demanded justice,
saying, "Your words soiled my
good name!"
"I'll take back what I said," replied
the sharp-tongued woman, "and
that will take away my guilt."
When the rabbi heard this, he knew
that this woman truly did not
understand her crime.
And so he said to the woman, "Your
words will not be excused until you
have done the following. Bring my
feather pillow to the market square.
Cut it and let the feathers fly
through the air. Then collect every
one of the feathers from the pillow
and bring them all back to me.
When you have done this, you will
be absolved of your crime."

The woman agreed, but thought to herself, The old rabbi has finally gone mad!

She did as he asked, and cut the pillow. Feathers blew far and wide over the square and beyond. The wind carried them here and there, up into trees and under merchants' carts. She tried to catch them, but after much effort it was clear to her that she would never find them all.

She returned to the rabbi with only a few feathers in her hand. Facing the rabbi, she said, "I could not take back the feathers any more than I could take back my words. From now on I will be careful not to say anything that would harm another, for there is no way to control the flight of words, any more than I could control the flight of these feathers." From that day, the woman spoke kindly of all she met.

—A Hasidic tale from Eastern Europe

6.

I can make a difference

by persevering and not giving up.

"I think I can—I think I can—I think I can—I think I can—I think I can—I think I can—I think I can—I think I can—I think I can."

—*Watty Piper*, THE LITTLE ENGINE THAT COULD

Mother to Son

WELL, SON, I'll tell you,
Life for me ain't been no crystal stair.
It's had tacks in it,
And splinters,
And boards torn up,
And places with no carpet on the floor—
Bare.
But all the time
I'se been a-climbin' on,
And reachin' landin's,
And turnin' corners,
And sometimes goin' in the dark
Where there ain't been no light.
So, boy, don't you turn back.
Don't you set down on the steps
'Cause you finds it's kinder hard.
Don't you fall now—
For I'se still goin', honey,
I'se still climbin',
And life for me ain't been no crystal stair.

—Langston Hughes

The Lion's Whiskers

BIZUNESH, A woman of the Ethiopian highlands, married Gudina, a man of the lowlands. Gudina's first wife had died of a fever, and he had an eight-year-old son whose name was Segab. When Bizunesh went to the house of Gudina, she quickly saw that Segab was a very sad boy because he missed his mother so much.

In only a short time Bizunesh grew to love Segab as if he were her own son, and she tried to be a good mother. She mended all of Segab's clothes and bought him new shoes. She asked him what foods he liked best, and she always saved the choicest pieces of meat from the *wat* for Segab. But Segab did not thank her. He would not even look at her or talk to her.

Bizunesh and Segab were often alone together because Gudina was a merchant who traveled with mule caravans to distant places. Bizunesh worried that Segab would be lonely and tried especially hard to please him when his father was away. "I have always wanted a son," Bizunesh told Segab. "Now God has given me one. I love you very much." Often she tried to kiss him.

But always Segab would turn away from her, and once he shouted, "You are not my mother. I do not love you."

One day Segab ran away from the house and hid in the town market until his father came and found him. When Segab returned home, Bizunesh tried to take him in her arms, but he pulled away from her. He would not touch the bowl of delicious soup she had saved for him. Bizunesh cried all that night.

In the morning Bizunesh went to the hut of a famous wise man. She told the wise man about her new stepson who refused to love her, no matter how hard she tried to please him.

"You must make me a magic love powder," Bizunesh told the old man. "I will put it in Segab's food, and then he will love me."

The wise man was silent for several minutes. "I can do what you ask," he said at last. "But to make such a powder, I must have three whiskers from the ferocious lion who lives in the black-rock desert across the river. Bring the whiskers to me, and I will make the powder for you."

Bizunesh could hardly believe her ears. "How can I get the lion's whiskers?" she asked. "He will surely kill me."

"I cannot tell you how to get the whiskers," the wise man said to Bizunesh. "That is for you to decide. But I must have them before I can make the love powder."

Bizunesh walked sadly from the wise man's hut. She did not sleep a wink that night, but in the morning her mind was made up. Nothing was as important to her as winning Segab's love. She had to try to get three whiskers from the lion even if he ate her. Only then would the wise man make the magic love powder for her.

That very day Bizunesh carried a large piece of raw meat to the black-rock desert. At last she saw the lion standing on a large rock, watching her from a great distance. When the lion jumped from the rock and loped toward her, Bizunesh was terrified. She threw the meat on the ground and ran. Only when she reached the river did she stop and look back. She saw the lion standing over the meat she had dropped. She heard him roar before he began to eat.

Two days later Bizunesh went again to the black-rock desert with a big piece of meat. She saw the lion watching her from the same rock. This time she walked closer to him before the lion jumped down and started toward her. Bizunesh stood still for a moment and watched the lion approach. Then her fear overcame her, and she threw the meat down and ran. When she looked back, she saw the lion eating.

On the following day Bizunesh walked even closer to the lion. This time she placed the meat on the ground and walked slowly away. Before she had gone far, she stopped and watched as the lion came and ate the meat.

Day after day Bizunesh came closer. Finally, she left the meat only a few hundred feet from the lion. The great beast growled, but Bizunesh did not think it sounded like an angry growl. She moved only a few steps away before she stopped and watched the lion eat. The next day Bizunesh left the meat fifty feet from the lion and stayed while he came and ate.

Then a few days later Bizunesh walked right up to the lion and handed him the meat. Her heart pounded with fear, but her love for Segab was so great that she did not run.

She watched the lion's great jaws fly open! Crash shut! She heard the sound of his teeth tearing through the meat. After a moment she reached out with a very sharp knife and cut three whiskers from the lion's muzzle. The lion was so busy eating that he did not even notice.

Bizunesh ran all the way to the wise man's hut. She was out of breath, but she was still able to shout, "I have the lion's whiskers!" She waved them in front of the old wise man. "Now make me the love powder, and Segab will surely love me."

The wise man took the lion's whiskers. He looked at them and then handed them back to Bizunesh. "You do not need a love powder," he told her. "You learned how to approach the lion—slowly. Do the same with Segab, and he will learn to love you."

—A tale from Ethiopia

7.

I can make a difference

by being determined and resourceful.

You must not expect anything from others. It's you, of yourself, of whom you must ask a lot. Only from oneself has one the right to ask everything and anything. This way it's up to you—your own choices—what you get from others remains a present, a gift!

—*Albert Schweitzer*

The Crow and the Pitcher

ONE HOT summer day, a crow was thirsty, so thirsty, in fact, that he felt he would die if he didn't have a cool drink of water. He came upon a tall pitcher, half full of water. The crow perched on the rim and leaned deep into the pitcher, but his beak was not long enough to reach the water. The crow was thirstier than ever now, with cool water so close and yet just out of reach. The crow thought for a moment and sprang into action.

Beneath the windowsill where the pitcher stood was a pile of pebbles. The crow flew down and picked up as many as he could carry. He dropped the pebbles into the pitcher. He repeated this several times, and every time he did, the level of the water rose just a little bit. After many trips, the water nearly reached the top. The crow was then able to drink his fill.

Where there's a will, there's a way.

—Aesop

Necessity

ONCE THERE was a farmer who was blessed with all a farmer could wish for: fine, fertile lands, happy, healthy animals, a comfortable home, and a handsome son, Petr. Petr was a good-natured young man and as loving a son as ever a father could wish for. But because everything went so well on the farm, he knew nothing at all of hardship and want.

His father worried about that. "Petr has never experienced even the slightest bit of ill luck. I don't even know if he could be clever enough to fend for himself if something went wrong! No, no, this will never do. I must find a way to test my boy and see if he can, indeed, overcome some hardship," he said to himself.

From that day on, the farmer gave Petr all the difficult jobs to do, all the tasks that might possibly go wrong. But nothing went wrong!

"This will never do," the farmer mused. "I must find some way to test Petr."

He thought about it and thought about it. Then, late one night, the farmer woke with a laugh. "Ha! I have it! I know exactly how I'll test my Petr."

So the next morning he called his son to him and said, "Petr, I wish you to go on an errand for me."

"Of course, Father. What is it you need?" the son replied.

"I wish you to go into the forest and look for necessity."

Petr frowned. He assumed his father meant for him to go and find a person. But Necessity! That was an odd name for anyone to bear. "And where will I find Mr. Necessity?"

"Don't worry, my boy. If you don't find necessity, necessity will surely find you and teach you a wise lesson. But I don't want you to come home before that happens. Do you understand? You are not to come home until you have found necessity or necessity has found you."

Now Petr was more confused than before. Was the mysterious Necessity a friend of his father's?

Whoever he was, he must be a clever fellow indeed, if he could find someone in that vast forest! "Very well, Father," Petr said reluctantly. "Let me take a horse and—"

"No, no," his father interrupted. "We need all the horses today."

"Then I shall take a sturdy oxcart and—"

"No, no, we shall need all the sturdy oxcarts as well. Here is what you may take."

He led the boy to the most rickety, most worn-out oxcart on the whole farm. "This?" Petr asked. "B-but it will surely fall apart the moment I enter the forest."

"Don't worry," his father said with a smile. "If it does fall apart, necessity will help you fix it."

And so a truly puzzled Petr drove his two oxen off into the forest, the rickety old cart rocking and creaking beneath him. He drove far and long into the forest,

till the tall trees nearly shut out the light with their leaves and he could barely see his way. And all the time he rode, Petr called out: "Mr. Necessity? Mr. Necessity? Can you hear me? Please, Mr. Necessity, I'm looking for you!"

But no one answered. The day wore on, and the night came near, and Petr looked around uneasily. The forest was a very wild place, full of wolves and bears that might want to eat a team of oxen. Or even a boy!

"Mr. Necessity! Please!"

Just then, the oxcart struck a rock and tilted sideways so suddenly that Petr was thrown to the ground. As he picked himself up, the boy groaned.

"Look at this cart. One of the axles has snapped right in half, and there's the wheel, rolled off by itself." Petr glanced around with a shiver. He was alone, all alone in the middle of the wild forest. *And there isn't a glimpse of Mr. Necessity. Now what am I going to do?* the boy wondered to himself.

He sat down on a rock, with his head in his hands, until the oxen, who had been peacefully nibbling on leaves, straightened up with a snort. Petr straightened, too. What was that? Had he heard wolves howling?

"I can't stay here and wait for Mr. Necessity. Father was wrong; he's nowhere

around. I can't walk all the way home, not with the night almost here. So I'll just have to fix the cart myself. But how?"

Petr walked around the cart. The wheels looked all right, but the axle was definitely broken.

"There are many stray branches lying around. I wonder . . . ," Petr thought aloud. He used his belt knife to whittle off a good, straight branch that looked to be the right size.

"Now, how do I hoist the cart up so that I can get the broken axle off and the new one on?" He paused and then said, "I think I know."

Petr took another branch, a strong, springy one. He balanced it on a rock, slipped one end of the branch under the cart, and stood on the other end. Sure enough, the branch acted as a lever, and the cart bed came up off the ground. Petr braced the branch with another rock, so the cart wouldn't fall on him, and set about pulling off the broken axle and slipping in the new one. He fixed both wheels firmly onto the new axle, then let the cart settle back to the ground.

"It worked! The new axle is holding!"

Petr jumped back onto the cart and picked up the reins. "Come, my oxen. Let's go home!"

Meanwhile, Petr's father was pacing back and forth, forth and back. Had he done the right thing, sending his boy off into the forest? Here it was, nearly night, and there wasn't a sign of the boy.

Ah, but here he comes! Here comes Petr now! The father looked at the newly repaired cart and beamed. "My boy, my clever, clever boy, you did find necessity!"

Petr frowned. "I did no such thing. I saw no one in the forest at all, most certainly not any Mr. Necessity. And he didn't teach me a thing! All I learned was that if something needs to be done, you cannot just wait around for someone else to do it. You have to help yourself."

The farmer laughed. "My dear boy, I never meant for you to find a *man* named Necessity! I just wanted to be sure you could solve problems by yourself. And now I can be proud because necessity has taught you a fine lesson after all."

—*A tale from Romania*

Albert Schweitzer

8.

I can make a difference

by being grateful for the gift

and wonders of life.

Just to be is a blessing. Just to live is holy.

—*Rabbi Abraham Joshua Heschel*

The greatest thing is to give thanks for everything.
He who has learned this knows what it means to live.
He has penetrated the whole mystery of life:
giving thanks for everything.

—*Albert Schweitzer*

From *Leaves of Grass*

. . . I KNOW NOTHING else but miracles,

Whether I walk the streets of Manhattan,

Or dart my sight over the roofs of houses toward the sky,

Or wade with naked feet along the beach just in the edge of the water,

Or stand under trees in the woods,

Or talk by day with any one I love, or sleep in bed at night with anyone I love,

Or sit at table at dinner with the rest,

Or look at strangers opposite me riding in the car,

Or watch honey-bees busy around the hive of a summer forenoon,

Or animals feeding in the fields,

Or birds, or the wonderfulness of insects in the air,

Or the exquisite delicate thin curve of the new moon in spring.

These with the rest, one and all, are to me miracles,

The whole referring, yet each distinct and in its place.

To me every hour of the light and dark is a miracle,

Every cubic inch of space is a miracle,

Every square yard of the surface of the earth is spread with miracles,

Every foot of the interior swarms with miracles.

—Walt Whitman

Giving the Moon

On a clear and beautiful night, a monk sat in front of his hut in the countryside, gazing at the full moon. Basking in the glow of the moon, the monk did not hear a thief creeping up behind him.

"Give me all you own!" cried the thief.

The monk replied, "My hut is empty. My only possessions are these ragged clothes. Come sit here with me. I am happy to share the beauty of the night sky with you."

The thief was not interested. Again he cried, "Give me all you own," and so the monk removed his clothes and handed them over. The thief tucked them under his arm and left.

Gazing up at the moon once more, shivering in the chill night air, the monk watched the thief make his way down the mountain. With a sigh he said to himself, "What a poor man! I wish I could give him this beautiful moon."

—A Zen story from Japan

The Creation

AND GOD stepped out on space,
And he looked around and said:
I'm lonely—
I'll make me a world.

And far as the eye of God could see
Darkness covered everything,
Blacker than a hundred midnights
Down in a cypress swamp.

Then God smiled,
And the light broke,
And the darkness rolled up on one side,
And the light stood shining on the other,
And God said: That's good!

Then God reached out and took the light in His hands,
And God rolled the light around in His hands
Until He made the sun;
And He set that sun a-blazing in the heavens.
And the light that was left from making the sun
God gathered it up in a shining ball
And flung it against the darkness,
Spangling the night with the moon and stars.
Then down between
The darkness and the light
He hurled the world;
And God said: That's good!

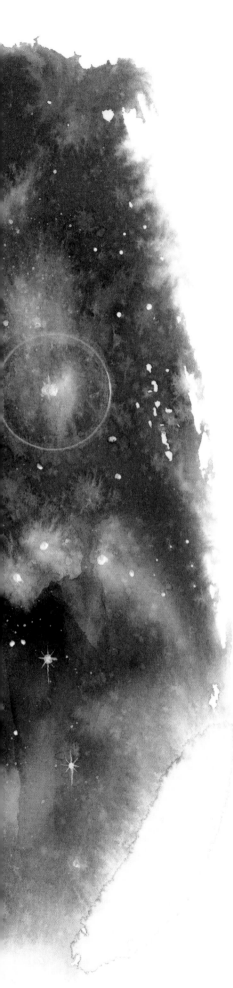

Then God himself stepped down—
And the sun was on His right hand,
And the moon was on His left;
The stars were clustered about His head,
And the earth was under His feet.
And God walked, and where He trod
His footsteps hollowed the valleys out
And bulged the mountains up.

Then He stopped and looked and saw
That the earth was hot and barren.
So God stepped over to the edge of the world
And He spat out the seven seas—
He batted His eyes, and the lightnings flashed—
He clapped His hands, and the thunders rolled—
And the waters above the earth came down,
The cooling waters came down.

Then the green grass sprouted,
And the little red flowers blossomed,
The pine tree pointed his finger to the sky,
And the oak spread out his arms,
The lakes cuddled down in the hollows of the ground,
And the rivers ran down to the sea;
And God smiled again,
And the rainbow appeared,
And curled itself around His shoulder.

Then God raised His arm and He waved His hand
Over the sea and over the land,
And He said: Bring forth! Bring forth!

And quicker than God could drop His hand,
Fishes and fowls
And beasts and birds
Swam the rivers and the seas,
Roamed the forests and the woods,
And split the air with their wings.
And God said: That's good!

Then God walked around,
And God looked around
On all that He had made.
He looked at His sun,
And He looked at His moon,
And He looked at His little stars;
He looked on His world
With all its living things,
And God said: I'm lonely still.

Then God sat down—
On the side of a hill where He could think;
By a deep, wide river He sat down;
With His head in His hands,
God thought and thought,
Till He thought: I'll make me a man!

Up from the bed of the river
God scooped the clay;
And by the bank of the river
He kneeled Him down;
And there the great God Almighty
Who lit the sun and fixed it in the sky,

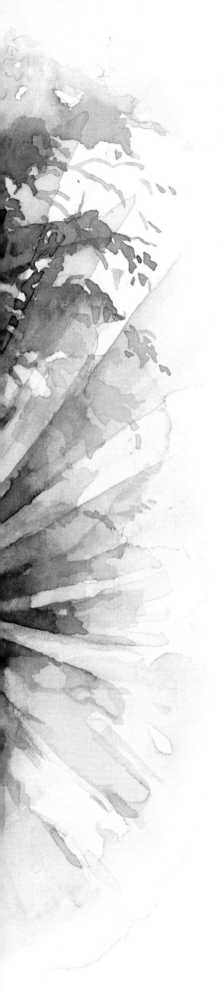

Who flung the stars to the most far corner of the night,
Who rounded the earth in the middle of His hand;
This Great God,
Like a mammy bending over her baby,
Kneeled down in the dust
Toiling over a lump of clay
Till He shaped it in His own image;

Then into it He blew the breath of life,
And man became a living soul.
Amen. Amen.

—*James Weldon Johnson*

9.

I can make a difference

by working together with others.

Drops that gather one by one finally become a sea.

—*Persian proverb*

Heaven and Hell

A CURIOUS MAN once asked to visit heaven and hell. Expecting hell to be a terrible, frightening place, he was amazed to find people seated around a lovely banquet table. The table was piled high with every delicious thing one could possibly want. The man thought, *Perhaps hell is not so bad after all.*

Looking closely, however, he noticed that everyone at the table was miserable.

They were starving, because, although there was a mountain of food before them, they had been given three-foot-long chopsticks. There was no way to carry the food to their mouths with such long chopsticks, and so no one could eat a bite.

The man was then taken to heaven. To his surprise, he found the exact same situation as he had seen in hell. People were gathered around a banquet table piled with food. All the diners held a pair of three-foot-long chopsticks in their hands. But here in heaven, everyone was happily eating the delicious food, for the residents of heaven were using their extra-long chopsticks to feed one another.

—A tale from China

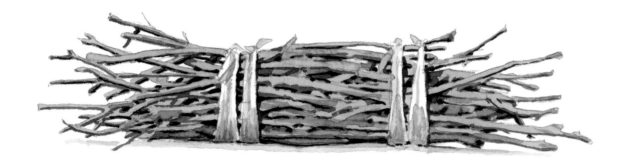

The Bundle of Sticks

DURING A TIME of war and famine, life was hard for all. One family of five sons made life even more difficult by fighting among themselves constantly. One day their father grew tired of their bickering. He spoke to them, asking, "When people around us are dying in battle and hunger, why must you act in such a way? Why can't you get along?" His words seemed to have no effect, so he instructed his eldest son to collect a bundle of sticks.

The eldest son did as he was asked and brought the bundle to his father. "Now break the sticks," his father commanded. The son, though strong, could not break the bundle. The second son tried and failed, as did the third and the fourth. When it was his turn, the fifth son untied the bundle and pulled out a single stick.

"Father," he said, "I know why you asked us to break this bundle. When we fight among ourselves, we are like this single stem"—and he snapped the stick in two— "and break easily. But when we stick together, we are impossible to defeat."

The father was happy to have raised such a wise son, and asked the older brothers to listen to him.

—*Aesop*

The Parts of the House Argue

HIGH UP in a nipa palm tree house, a large and quarrelsome family once lived. Not a day passed in the tree house without a disagreement of some kind. One day the family members began to quarrel about who was the most important member of the family. Soon the parts of the house began to argue about the same topic.

"I am the most important part," said one of the poles that held the house high off the ground. "I was the first pole driven into the ground. All the rest of you came after me."

The other poles disagreed. "Without us," one of them said, "you wouldn't be able to hold the house off the ground."

As the poles argued, the floor supports chimed in, "No one would care about the poles if we weren't here to hold you together!"

The cross supports called out, "Without us, you would all wobble and sag!"

The floor rumbled, "Without me, there's no reason for the rest of you!"

The bamboo walls rattled, "We make the rooms, and without rooms, this wouldn't even be a house!"

The roof beams and the ceiling and the palm leaf roof quarreled bitterly over which of them was the most important until, all at once, the many parts of the house realized that there was no way to win the argument, for each part was equally important. With one great breath the parts of the house sighed, "None is important without the other," and at that moment, the family members ceased quarreling as well. From that moment, the family lived together in peace.

—A tale from the Philippines

Swimmy

A HAPPY SCHOOL of little fish lived in a corner of the sea somewhere. They were all red. Only one of them was as black as a mussel shell. He swam faster than his brothers and sisters. His name was Swimmy.

One bad day a tuna fish, swift, fierce and very hungry, came darting through the waves. In one gulp he swallowed all the little red fish. Only Swimmy escaped.

He swam away in the deep wet world. He was scared, lonely and very sad.

But the sea was full of wonderful creatures, and as he swam from marvel to marvel Swimmy was happy again.

He saw a medusa made of rainbow jelly . . . a lobster, who walked about like a water-moving machine . . . strange fish, pulled by an invisible thread . . . a forest of seaweeds growing from sugar-candy rocks . . . an eel whose tail was almost too far away to remember . . . and sea anemones, who looked like pink palm trees swaying in the wind.

Then, hidden in the dark shade of rocks and weeds, he saw a school of little fish, just like his own.

"Let's go and swim and play and SEE things!" he said happily.

"We can't," said the little red fish. "The big fish will eat us all."

"But you can't just lie there," said Swimmy. "We must THINK of something."

Swimmy thought and thought and thought.

Then suddenly he said, "I have it! We are going to swim all together like the biggest fish in the sea!"

He taught them to swim close together, each in his own place, and when they had learned to swim like one giant fish, he said, "I'll be the eye."

And so they swam in the cool morning water and in the midday sun and chased the big fish away.

—Leo Lionni

Let us put our minds together and see what life
we can make for our children.

—*Sitting Bull*

Dr. George Washington Carver

10.

I can make a difference

by being compassionate and kind.

My religion is very simple. My religion is kindness.

—*The Dalai Lama*

Excerpt from a letter from the great scientist *George Washington Carver* to the Tuskegee class of 1922, dated January 9, 1922

As your father . . . I hope . . . each one of my children will rise to the full height of your possibilities, which means the possession of these eight cardinal virtues which constitutes a lady or a gentleman.

1st. Be clean both inside and outside.

2nd. Who neither looks up to the rich or down on the poor.

3rd. Who loses, if needs be, without squealing.

4th. Who wins without bragging.

5th. Who is always considerate of women, children and old people.

6th. Who is too brave to lie.

7th. Who is too generous to cheat.

8th. Who takes his share of the world and lets other people have theirs.

May God help you to carry out these eight cardinal virtues and peace and prosperity be yours through life.

Lovingly yours,
G. W. Carver

The Month of March

I N ITALY, long ago, there lived two brothers. The elder, Cianne, was as rich as any-one in the land. The younger, Lise, was poor. Although he was rich in material things, Cianne was poor in spirit, and he refused to give Lise as much as a single coin on which to live. As a result, Lise set off to make his fortune on his own.

After walking all day, a tired, wet, and cold Lise stopped at a humble inn. Inside he found twelve young men sitting around a blazing fire. Taking pity on Lise, they took him in out of the rainy and cold March night. Lise was happy to be inside, and as he warmed his hands, one of the young men watched him closely, with an annoyed look on his face. "What do you think of this weather?" he asked gruffly.

Lise was a thoughtful young man, and so he replied, "I think every month has a job to do, but men, being human, always want what they don't have. In the win-ter we complain about the cold, and in the summer we complain about the heat. If the months didn't do their duties, nature would be turned upside down. I say let us leave heaven to its course, and each month to its job."

The young man's cross expression brightened a little, but he continued in a rough voice: "Even so, you can't deny that March is a particularly awful month, with its cold rain and frost and even snow."

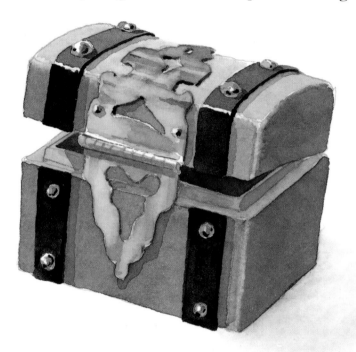

Lise did not agree. "We must appreciate March as the gateway to spring and all its bounty. Without March, we would not have the grass and apple blossoms and young flowers of April and May. March starts all life growing again, and for that, I appreciate it."

With that, the young man's face creased into a smile, for he was March, and the other eleven youths around the fire were his brothers. He was so grateful to Lise for seeing the good in him rather than the bad that he decided to reward him. March gave Lise a tiny box with the instruction that, should he ever want for something, he had only to ask for it and open the box. Lise thanked him, and they all went to sleep for the night.

Early the next morning, Lise continued his journey. It was a cold and snowy day, and so, after a tiring morning of walking through the snow, he opened the box and wished for a carriage. Instantly a carriage appeared. When he wished for new clothes, they appeared as well. Satisfied that this box would provide him with all that he would need, Lise set out for home again.

He called on his brother, who was amazed at the things Lise had acquired. Lise explained about his trip and his visit with the twelve young men. He told Cianne of the box that March gave him, but said nothing of their conversation.

The next day Cianne hurried to the inn, anxious to get a magic box for himself. At the inn, all was as Lise had described; the twelve young men were sitting around the fire. When the cross man asked Cianne the same question about the month of March, Cianne, who was still cold and wet from his journey, said, "March is the worst month of the year! I wish it could be dropped from the calendar."

March managed to control his anger and said nothing. The next morning, when Cianne was about to leave, March presented him with a whip and said, "Whenever you wish for something, say, 'Whip, give me a hundred,' and you shall receive your reward." Cianne was very pleased, for he felt that a whip was bound to be at least as generous as the box that his brother had been given.

He hurried home, and once he was in the privacy of his room, he said, "Whip, give me a hundred." At once the whip commenced striking him on his legs, his back, and his face. Lise heard his cries and rushed to Cianne's room.

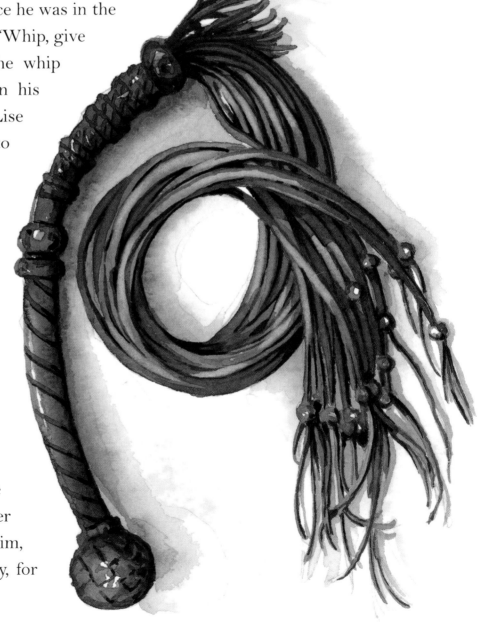

Cianne told him the story of how he came to have the whip. When he was through, Lise said, "You deserve what you got, for your cruel words and greedy nature have hurt many people. You should watch what you say, for you never know whom you may hurt with your words." But when he saw how dejected his brother looked, Lise took pity on him, and said, "But do not worry, for my box will provide enough for both of us, and I am happy to share. Let's forget the past and start again."

Cianne learned his lesson, for from that day on, he always spoke well of everyone, and his heart was full of love for all humankind.

—An Italian fairy tale

The Frog Prince

A LONG TIME AGO, there was a young princess who lived with her father the king. On a warm spring day, the princess sat by a well and amused herself bouncing a golden ball. She did this for hours, until the ball took an odd bounce and landed with a splash in the well. The princess began to cry, for she loved her ball, and there was no way that she could fetch it from the deep water of the well.

To her astonishment, a deep voice rumbled up from the depths of the well. "Why are you crying?" it asked. The princess called out that her ball had fallen into the well. Above the edge of the well, a large green frog appeared. It said, "If I return your ball to you, will you give me anything I want?"

"I will," replied the princess.

The frog did not want jewels or gold. He wanted only one thing: "I want to be your friend."

Without thinking, for she wanted her ball back, the princess agreed, and the frog retrieved her ball. Happy to have her ball back, the princess skipped away with only a brief nod of thanks to the frog.

That night at dinner, an anxious footman whispered in the king's ear, "There's a frog at the door, and he wishes to speak to the princess." The king was a jolly man, and he thought this was quite funny. When the princess told him the story, however, and described her promise to the frog, his smile faded. He was not only jolly, he was just, and the king explained to the princess that she must keep her word. The frog was brought to the table and a place was laid for him.

After dinner, the princess and the frog went to her room to play. When it was time for bed, the frog jumped up on the princess's fluffy bed. The princess was not happy. "You are a fat and slimy frog," she said, "and you'll ruin my bed. You cannot sleep on it."

With that the frog began to weep. "All I wanted," he whispered between sobs, "was to be your friend. But you think I am fat and slimy. You aren't my friend at all."

The princess took pity on the frog. "Oh, frog, what shall we do with you?" she said, and gave him a kiss.

In a flash, the frog turned into a sturdy young prince with bright eyes and a brilliant smile. He explained that a witch had cast a spell on him that could only be undone by the kiss of a beautiful girl. The princess and her good heart had released him from the spell.

The princess and her prince fell in love and were married. They lived lives of great happiness together, full of kindness to all, even those who seemed least deserving of it.

—The Brothers Grimm

11.

I can make a difference

by being nonviolent

and working for peace.

Blessed are the peacemakers:
for they shall be called the children of God.

—*Matthew 5:9*

The Quarrel

I QUARRELED with my brother,
I don't know what about,
One thing led to another
And somehow we fell out.
The start of it was slight,
The end of it was strong,
He said he was right,
I knew he was wrong!

We hated one another.
The afternoon turned black.
Then suddenly my brother
Thumped me on the back,
And said, "Oh, *come* along!
We can't go on all night—
I was in the wrong."
So he was in the right.

—*Eleanor Farjeon*

Little Girls Wiser Than Their Elders

EASTER WAS EARLY. Folks had just ceased going in sledges. The snow still lay in the courtyards, and little streams ran through the village. In an alley between two dvors (*courts*) a large pool had collected from the dung heaps. And near this pool were standing two little girls from either dvor, one of them younger, the other older.

The mothers of the two little girls had dressed them in new sarafans (*jumpers*), the younger one's blue, the elder's of yellow flowered damask. Both wore red handkerchiefs. The little girls, after mass was over, had gone to the pool, shown each other their dresses, and begun to play. And the whim seized them to splash in the water. The younger one was just going to wade into the pool with her little slippers on, but the older one said:

"Don't do it, Malashka. Your mother will scold. I'm going to take off my shoes and stockings. You take off yours."

The little girls took off their shoes and stockings, held up their clothes, and went into the pool so as to meet. Malashka waded in up to her ankles, and said:

"It's deep, Akulyushka. I am afraid."

"Nonsense! It won't be any deeper. Come straight toward me."

They approached nearer and nearer to each other. And Akulka said:

"Be careful, Malashka, don't splash, but go more slowly."

But the words were hardly out of her mouth, when Malashka put her foot down into the water; it splashed directly on Akulka's sarafan. The sarafan was well spattered, and the water flew into her nose and eyes.

Akulka saw the spots on her sarafan; she became angry with Malashka, scolded her, ran after her, tried to slap her.

Malashka was frightened when she saw what mischief she had done; she sprang out of the pool and hastened home.

Akulka's mother happened to pass by and saw her little daughter's sarafan spattered, and her shirt bedaubed.

"How did you get yourself all covered with dirt, you little good-for-nothing?"

"Malashka spattered me on purpose."

Akulka's mother caught Malashka, and struck her on the back of the head.

Malashka howled along the whole street. Malashka's mother came out.

"What are you striking my daughter for?"

She began to scold her neighbor. A word for a word, the women got into a quarrel. The muzhiks (*peasants*) hastened out; a great crowd gathered on the street. All were screaming. No one would listen to anyone. They quarreled, and the one jostled the other; there was a general row imminent; but an old woman, Akulka's grandmother, interfered.

She came out into the midst of the muzhiks, and began to speak.

"What are you doing, neighbors? What day is it? We ought to rejoice. And you are doing such wrong things!"

They did not heed the old woman; they almost struck her. And the old woman would never have succeeded in persuading them, had it not been for Akulka and

Malashka. While the women were keeping up the quarrel, Akulka cleaned her sarafanchik and came out again to the pool in the alley. She picked up a little stone, and began to clear away the earth by the pool, so as to let the water run into the street.

While she was cleaning it out, Malashka also came along and began to help her—to make a little gutter with a splinter.

The muzhiks were just coming to blows when the water reached the street, flowing through the gutter made by the little girls; and it went straight to the very spot where the old woman was trying to separate the muzhiks.

The little girls were chasing it, one on one side, the other on the other, of the runnel.

"Hold it back, Malashka! Hold it!" cried Akulka. Malashka also tried to say something, but she laughed so that she could not speak.

Thus the little girls were chasing it, and laughing as the splinter swam down the runnel.

They ran right into the midst of the muzhiks. The old woman saw them, and she said to the muzhiks:

"You should fear God, you muzhiks! It was on account of these same little girls that you picked a quarrel, but they forgot all about it long ago; dear little things, they are playing together lovingly again."

The muzhiks looked at the little girls and felt ashamed. Then the muzhiks laughed at themselves, and went home to their dvors.

"If ye are not like little children, ye cannot enter into the kingdom of God."

—*Leo Tolstoy*

How War Was Ended

FIVE HUNDRED YEARS before the first outsiders arrived in central Alaska, there was a fierce Yup'ik warrior named Aganugpak. All of his people knew him to be the bravest and strongest warrior of his time. His skill with harpoon and bow and arrow was legendary.

Aganugpak lived during a time of misery and war. All across the icy tundra, warring groups fought. Blood was shed daily, and people lived in constant fear of attack. The Yup'ik people lived in underground houses carved from the dirt and protected from the cold by thick layers of sod. The smoke from their cooking fires drifted up and out through holes cut in the ground. During this time roving bands of warriors traveled with "smellers," men with such keen senses of smell that they could detect a cooking fire from miles away. These smellers would lead the warriors to the underground homes, and they would attack the people living there. Soon people were afraid to light fires. They lived in the cold and the dark, eating what they could. They were hungry and afraid.

After some time Aganugpak had a vision. In his mind he saw the houses in his village in burning ruins. He saw a lake of blood, blood drained from the warriors of his people. Aganugpak saw the ghosts of dead warriors rise up from their graves and do battle with the living.

As he watched this vision unfold before him, this brave warrior knew that war cannot be won. No matter how fearless the warrior, the result of war could only be more suffering.

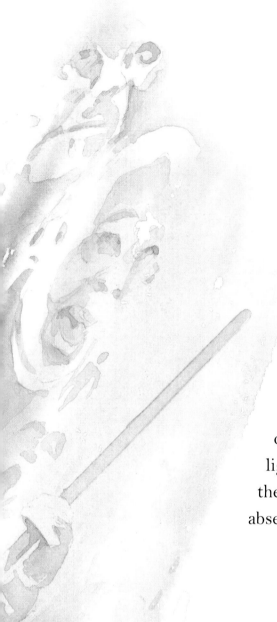

Aganugpak decided that war must end. The Yup'ik people were astonished when their greatest warrior announced that he would no longer use his harpoon and bow and arrow to cause death to another person, but they trusted and respected him. The Yup'ik people put down their weapons. War was ended for all time.

The Yup'ik created new ways to solve their differences. When people disagreed, they participated in singing contests and dancing contests, and they found clever ways to insult one another. These contests were held in front of the entire community, and so they brought people together while settling disputes. Peace came to the land. People were able to light their hearth fires, warm their homes, and cook their meals. People were able to prosper and grow in the absence of war.

—A central Yup'ik Eskimo tale from the
North American Arctic

If I Had a Hammer

If I HAD a hammer, I'd hammer in the morning,
I'd hammer in the evening all over this land;
I'd hammer out danger, I'd hammer out a warning,
I'd hammer out love between my brothers and my sisters,
All over this land.

If I had a bell, I'd ring it in the morning,
I'd ring it in the evening all over this land;
I'd ring out danger, I'd ring out a warning,
I'd ring out love between my brothers and my sisters,
All over this land.

If I had a song, I'd sing it in the morning,
I'd sing it in the evening all over this land.
I'd sing out danger, I'd sing out a warning,
I'd sing out love between my brothers and my sisters,
All over this land.

Well, I got a hammer, and I've got a bell,
And I've got a song all over this land.
It's the hammer of justice, it's the bell of freedom,
It's the song about love between my brothers and my sisters,
All over this land.

—Lee Hays and Pete Seeger

If I Had a Hammer

Words and Music:
Lee Hays and Pete Seeger

With conviction

If I had a ham - mer, _____ I'd ham - mer in the

morn - ing, _____ I'd ham - mer in the eve - ning, _____

__ all o - ver this land, _____ I'd ham - mer out

dan - ger, I'd ham - mer out a warn - ing,

I'd __ ham - mer out love be - tween my broth - ers and my sis - ters,

All _____ o - ver this land. _____

Nonviolence is the weapon of the strong.

—*Mahatma Gandhi*

We shall find peace. We shall hear the angels, we shall see the sky sparkling with diamonds.

—*Anton Pavlovich Chekhov*

Mother Teresa

12.

I can make a difference

by being faithful and struggling

for what I believe.

God has not called me to be successful. He has called me to be faithful.

—*Mother Teresa*

The more unpropitious the situation in which we demonstrate hope, the deeper the hope is. [Hope is] not the conviction that something will turn out well, but the certainty that something makes sense regardless of how it turns out. It is also this hope, above all, which gives us the strength to live and continually to try new things, even in conditions that seem as hopeless as ours do, here and now.

—*Václav Havel*

King Solomon's Ring

OF ALL King Solomon's servants, the bravest and most faithful was Benaiah, the captain of the guard. He had been the king's companion in the fabulous adventures of his earlier days and more than once had saved his master's life. He had never failed in any task that Solomon had set him.

This, indeed, was his only boast; for Benaiah was a man of action, not fond of talking. When he was not on duty guarding the king, he would sit among the courtiers so silent that they made the mistake of thinking him dull. They would tease him; but Benaiah, sure of his place with the king, paid no attention to them.

Once, however, Solomon himself took part in a mischievous trick they were playing on his faithful follower. "Benaiah," he said one Sabbath evening early in spring, "you are fond of saying that you have never failed in any task for me."

Benaiah bowed respectfully. "That is my only boast, O King."

"Then let me put you to one more test. I want you to find me a certain wonderful ring, so that I can wear it at the Succoth festival. That will give you six months for the search."

"If the ring exists under heaven, my lord, you shall have it! But tell me, I pray, what makes it so precious?"

"It has magic powers," said the king. "If a happy man looks at it, he at once becomes downcast and gloomy; but if a person in misery or mourning beholds it, hope rises in his heart and he is comforted." Now King Solomon knew that there was no such ring. But he met Benaiah's eager gaze with a smile of encouragement.

"You shall wear it at the Succoth feast," Benaiah exclaimed, "if there be any strength left in me!"

He could hardly wait for the Sabbath to be over, so that he could start on his quest.

First he went to the finest jewelers and goldsmiths and silversmiths in Jerusalem, for he didn't know whether the ring was of silver or gold, set with precious stones or plain. To each man he described its qualities, but no one knew anything about it. They had not even heard of such a ring. Benaiah also tried the smaller shops and less prosperous dealers. Always he met with the same raised eyebrows, the same shake of the head.

Ah, this ring must be treasured in some far-off city, thought Benaiah.

When the great caravans came southward from Babylon and Damascus and Tyre, he was the first to meet them, and he spoke to the traders of precious gems, and said: "I am seeking a ring with this magical quality: When a happy person looks at it, he becomes sad; and when a wretched man beholds it, he ceases to grieve and is comforted. Do you have it? I will pay any price. It is for my lord, King Solomon."

These widely traveled merchants also shook their heads. Each told him, "I regret, Captain, that I have no such ring. It may not even exist, for I have never heard of it. I have other rare jewels that will surely please—"

"Look for this ring, I pray you," said Benaiah firmly. "If you have it for me on your return journey, you may name your own price."

He went to Beersheba in the south, to meet the caravans that came up from the cities of Egypt, and from Yemen, the land of perfumes. He asked the jewel merchants: "Can you find me a ring which has the wonderful powers of changing a man's grief to joy when he beholds it? Also, it changes happiness to sorrow at a glance."

"Wonderful, indeed!" they answered, "if such a ring exists. But we have not heard of it."

"It exists," said Benaiah. "My lord, King Solomon, wishes for it. You shall have any price you ask if you bring me that ring on your return."

He went down to Jaffa, where the ships came in from the Great Sea and the Ocean of Darkness, in the west, and the Spice Islands and the Land of Ophir, to the east and south. To each merchant he said, "I seek a magic ring. It makes a mourner forget his grief, when he looks at it; but when a happy man sees it, his heart sinks and there is no joy in him. I will pay a great price for it."

And each one answered him, "I know of no such ring. You are the first to tell me of it."

"Then seek it, in all lands where you travel. For if you bring it to me on your return, you may ask what you wish in payment."

Benaiah thought, How wise is my lord, the king! He knows the things hidden from other men, even at the ends of the earth!

Meanwhile weeks, then months, went by. It was summer. The caravans returned from the north. None of the merchants brought him the ring, or even any word of where it might be found. The caravans came again from the south. "We would gladly help you," the dealers said, "but in all the cities and the markets where we sought it, we have seen no such ring. Nor have we heard tell of it."

Summer was over. One by one the ships returned from prosperous voyages over calm waters, and each of the sea captains and the merchant-adventurers told Benaiah the same disheartening tale. They had not seen such a ring. No one had heard of it.

The last harvest of the year, and with it the Succoth festival, was approaching. Every time King Solomon saw Benaiah, he would say: "Well, how goes the search,

Benaiah? Have you found the ring?" And when Benaiah shook his head, Solomon said with a pleasant smile, "Search diligently, Benaiah. You will surely find it."

"With God's help!" Benaiah said.

But as the days went by and brought no good news, he began to avoid the places where he might meet the king.

Now it was only a week before Succoth. There was no more hope in Benaiah's heart. He could not eat and his nights were sleepless. He dreaded the moment when he must tell the king he had failed. He did not mind so much that the clever young courtiers would laugh at him. But he could not bear to have the king's trust in him shaken.

It was the last night before Succoth Eve. Benaiah lay restless on his bed for several hours; then he rose and dressed and walked about the silent city, hardly knowing where he went. He wandered away from the palace, and the fine houses of the courtiers and those who served the king, through the neighborhoods where the plain people lived.

Night faded from the sky and the east brightened with the rosy fire of dawn as Benaiah went downward from street to street, until he reached the bottom of the valley between the two hills on which Jerusalem was built.

Benaiah looked about him. It was a poor street, with small, shabby houses. As the sun rose, people in patched and faded garments came out of their dwellings and set about the morning's business.

Benaiah saw a young man spread a mat upon the moss-grown paving-stones in front of his home, and arrange on it some baskets of silver and turquoise trinkets and mother-of-pearl beads such as people without much money could afford.

Shall I ask here? thought Benaiah. What use, when even the most famous travelers have never heard of the ring? Still, it will only mean another no.

He approached the jeweler. "I want a ring," he said, repeating words that had lost their meaning for him. "A wonderful ring. It has magic powers. When a happy man looks at it, he becomes sad. When a grieving person sees it, he becomes joyful. Do you have it?"

The young man shook his

head. "This is a poor little place, O Captain, and we know nothing of such marvels. . . ."

Benaiah walked away.

But meanwhile the jeweler's old grandfather had come out to sit by the doorway in the early sunshine. He beckoned the young man to him and whispered in his ear.

"Wait, Captain!" the jeweler called out, "I think we can serve you." Hardly able to believe his ears, Benaiah turned back.

The young man took from one of his baskets a plain gold ring, such as is used for weddings. With a sharp tool he engraved something on it and laid it in the captain's hand.

Benaiah looked at it, then he laughed aloud. His heart filled with joy. He had not been so happy since the day he had first started the search. "This is the ring!" he cried, and gave the young jeweler all the money in his purse. "Come to the palace and you shall have more," he added, "for I cannot thank you enough."

He hurried back to his house but was too impatient to sleep. However, he kept out of the king's sight, not to betray his happy secret until the right time should come. He bathed and made ready for the festival. Then in his finest holiday attire he took his place at the banquet table.

He enjoyed the feast, for now that his duty was done he could pay attention to such matters as food and drink. He laughed at every joke, and thought kindly of the clever young courtiers.

When the merriment was at its height, King Solomon turned to Benaiah. A hush spread around the table. "Now, my faithful Captain," the king exclaimed mirthfully, "where is the famous ring?" Of course, after he and the courtiers had laughed for a while at Benaiah's simplicity, Solomon meant to tell him that he had not failed, for no such ring existed.

But to Solomon's astonishment, Benaiah cried: "I have

it, O King! It is here." And, almost stumbling in his haste to reach the king's side, he placed it on Solomon's hand.

As the king looked at it, the teasing laughter faded from his face. He became silent and thoughtful, for the magic of the ring was working. The jeweler had engraved on it three Hebrew letters, *Gimmel, Zayin, Yud,* standing for the words *Gam Zeh Ya'avor*—"This, too, shall pass." Thus King Solomon was sharply reminded that all his glory, and the beauty and splendor with which he was surrounded, must crumble away into dust, leaving him nothing but an old memory and a tale that is told.

When he raised his eyes again, they met Benaiah's eyes with a humbled, grateful look. He was ashamed of the trick he had played on his loyal follower.

"Benaiah," he said, "you are wiser than I thought you. This is a wonderful gift. I will wear it on the same finger as my signet." He drew from his hand a ring with a precious ruby. "And you in turn must wear this ruby, so that all men may know you as the king's friend.

—A traditional Jewish tale

Issun Boschi, the Inchling

ON A ROCKY, windswept island far from the mainland of Japan, an old couple lived together. They had been married for many years and were happy but for one thing: they had no children. Every morning they would pray to the Sun in the heavens for a child, but the Sun chose not to grant their wish.

For years they prayed and hoped, and finally the Sun rewarded them with a child—a baby boy. The boy was handsome and healthy, but he was no bigger than the man's thumb, and so the couple named him Issun Boschi, which means "the Inchling."

As he grew older, Issun Boschi stayed as small as a thumb, but he was also smart and very brave. When he was a young man, Issun Boschi decided he must travel to the city to make his fortune.

His parents did not want him to go, for they would miss him, and they feared for his safety. But being wise parents, they knew that they could not hold back their son. So they prepared him for his journey with a chopstick for a walking stick, a needle for a sword, and a rice bowl for a hat, and they wove a blade of grass into a neat little sheath for his needle-sword.

It is not easy to travel when one is no taller than a thumb, and so Issun Boschi walked with great determination, avoiding any danger along the way. When he reached a great river, he cleverly turned his rice bowl into a boat, his chopstick into an oar, and quickly made it across the river.

But a city is not a safe place for an inchling. Issun Boschi scrambled and darted out of the way of wagon wheels and clumsy dogs and troublemaking cats until he came to the most beautiful gate he had ever seen—the gate to the lord's palace. As he stopped to marvel at its splendor, a large boot came down from above, trapping him beneath it. Peeking out from the space between the heel and the sole, Issun Boschi called out to the owner of the boot with all his strength, "Hello! I'm down here!" The boot belonged to the lord of the city, who was concerned for the safety of the tiny man, so he took Issun Boschi into his palace.

Before long the lord and his family were enthralled by this charming young man. Issun Boschi loved to entertain the lord by dancing on his fan and dueling a

fly with his needle. He lived with the lord and became fast friends with the lord's daughter, a happy, bright young girl.

One day Issun Boschi went with the princess to visit a famous temple. On the way home they were ambushed by a green demon, a black demon, and a red demon bearing a magic hammer.

Issun Boschi moved quickly. With a fierce cry, he dove at the black demon and plunged his needle into the demon's eyes again and again. When the black demon fell, Issun Boschi turned to the green demon and did the same. Finally only the red demon was left. With a terrifying roar, he leaped for Issun Boschi, his horrible mouth open wide. Issun Boschi scrambled right into the gaping mouth and drove his needle into the demon's gums. Not even a demon could withstand such an assault, and so he fled without taking his magic hammer.

Issun Boschi, exhausted from his battle, picked himself up off the ground and presented the magic hammer to the princess. In a quiet voice, he said, "Make a wish, Your Highness, and it shall come true." But the princess insisted that Issun Boschi make the wish.

Issun Boschi looked up and said, "My wish is that my height would be equal to my love for the princess." At once, Issun Boschi was turned into a man who towered over all others.

The princess and Issun Boschi were married. They lived happily in the palace for many years with the lord and Issun Boschi's elderly parents.

—A tale from Japan

This Little Light of Mine

THIS LITTLE light of mine,
I'm goin' to let it shine.
This little light of mine,
I'm goin' to let it shine.
This little light of mine,
I'm goin' to let it shine.
Let it shine,
Let it shine,
Let it shine.

Everywhere I go,
I'm goin' to let it shine.
Everywhere I go,
I'm goin' to let it shine.
Everywhere I go,
I'm goin' to let it shine.
Let it shine,
Let it shine,
Let it shine.

All through the night,
I'm goin' to let it shine.
All through the night,
I'm goin' to let it shine.
All through the night,
I'm goin' to let it shine.
Let it shine,
Let it shine,
Let it shine.

God gave it to me, now
I'm goin' to let it shine.
God gave it to me, now
I'm goin' to let it shine.
God gave it to me, now
I'm goin' to let it shine.
Let it shine,
Let it shine,
Let it shine.

—*A traditional Negro spiritual*